QUEEN OF FLIES

Titles in Papercuts:

THE TRICK
KATE ORMAND

SCISSOR MAN
TIM COLLINS

QUEEN OF FLIES
TIM COLLINS

ALICE
DANNY PEARSON

THE SICKNESS
JACQUELINE RAYNER

A LITTLE SECRET
ANN EVANS

Badger Publishing Limited, Oldmedow Road, Hardwick Industrial Estate,
King's Lynn PE30 4JJ

Telephone: 01438 791037

www.badgerlearning.co.uk

QUEEN OF FLIES

TIM COLLINS | JAMES LAWRENCE

"All hail the Queen of Flies."

Queen of Flies ISBN 978-1-78837-218-3

Text © Tim Collins 2018
Complete work © Badger Publishing Limited 2018

Publisher: Susan Ross
Senior Editor: Danny Pearson
Editorial Coordinator: Claire Morgan
Copyeditor: Cheryl Lanyon
Designer: Bigtop Design Ltd
Illustration: James Lawrence

2 4 6 8 10 9 7 5 3 1

CHAPTER 1
THE QUEENS

"Don't tell me you want to make friends with the Queens," said Jess.

She grabbed a handful of crisps and shoved them into her mouth.

Mia shrugged. "I'm just curious," she said.

She wasn't just curious about the Queens. She was obsessed. There was Lauren, a tall girl with long, blonde hair and a fake smile. There was Savannah, who dyed her hair black and looked like she should be hanging around in a graveyard somewhere. And there was Gabriella, who wore a loose jumper.

"You're wasting your time," said Jess.

She tipped her head back and poured the last of the crisps into her mouth. Salty fragments tumbled down onto her jumper.

"They'll never talk to you," said Jess through a mouthful of greasy crisps.

Mia wondered why Jess was so certain. Maybe she was just afraid of losing her as a friend.

When she'd joined the school two months ago, the seat next to Jess had been one of only four free ones. A broad grin had spread across her face when Mia had chosen it.

But Jess didn't need to worry. Mia didn't want to join the Queens, she just wanted to talk to them and get a closer look. She thought she'd seen something the day before. It was something impossible. Something she couldn't have seen. Yet she was sure of it.

"You're talking about them like they're the school bullies," Mia said, sweeping her long red hair back behind her ears. "They don't seem so mean."

"It's not that," said Jess. "They just won't let anyone into their circle. And I've seen loads of people try."

The Queens were huddled together at the side of the Science block, talking quietly to each other.

"Come with me," Mia said, beckoning Jess forwards. "It might be easier with two of us."

"No way," said Jess, stepping back. "I sat next to them on the Geography field trip and they blanked me the whole time. I asked, like, a million questions but they said nothing at all."

Over by the Science block, Lauren was flicking her hair. Mia stared at her but she couldn't see clearly enough. She needed to be nearer.

"Maybe they're just shy," said Mia. "I'm going to give them a try."

"OK," said Jess. "But don't come back here when you crash and burn. I won't be here."

Mia strolled across the playground. Jess folded her arms and sulked but she stayed where she was.

Mia thought it was like the Queens had an invisible shield around them. Even the year seven kids, who usually bumped into everyone as they chased each other, steered clear.

The Queens stopped talking and watched Mia as she approached.

"Hi," she said, staring at Lauren's hair. "What are you guys up to?"

Lauren flashed her false smile. "We were just having a conversation."

Savannah scowled and put her hands on her hips. Gabriella looked down at the ground, adjusting the left side of her sweater.

"What about?" asked Mia. "It might be something I can help you with."

The Queens said nothing.

Mia glanced over her shoulder at Jess, who was smirking and shaking her head. A couple of younger kids had stopped to look too. Her social shame was fun to watch. But she didn't care.

"So you're all in my History class, right?" Mia asked. "What do you make of Mr Davies? Ever heard a voice that boring before?"

Lauren was still smiling but her eyes were blank. Gabriella was gazing at the concrete below her feet like it was the most interesting thing she'd ever seen.

Mia looked over her shoulder again. A few more students had stopped to stare.

"So, did you guys see anything good on TV last night?" asked Mia.

Now even Lauren dropped her smile. She turned her back to Mia and exchanged glances with Savannah and Gabriella.

Mia sighed. Now she'd have to skulk back to Jess and hear about how right she'd been.

She was about to go when Lauren flicked her hair. Mia was right behind her and if there had been anything underneath she'd have seen it. But there was nothing.

Mia's heart sank. It meant she'd imagined it yesterday.

She stomped back across the playground, her shoulders slumped, and planted her hands in her pockets.

The best thing now would be to forget about the Queens and move on. But how could she forget what she'd seen?

The day before, she'd been walking home from school. The Queens had been a few paces ahead, talking quietly as usual.

Lauren had flicked her hair and Mia had seen something that had made her feel sick and dizzy.

There had been an eyeball underneath Lauren's hair. A human eye, blue like Lauren's, but sore and bloodshot. There was no socket or eyelid, it was just a single eyeball hanging from a vein like an apple on a branch.

Mia had stared at it with her mouth open, feeling bile rise from her stomach. The eye had stared back. She'd thought she'd seen an expression of sheer hatred in it. But a second later it had been covered by Lauren's hair again.

Now it seemed it had never existed at all.

CHAPTER 2
THE INJURY

Mia tried to force the image of the stray eyeball from her mind. And she managed it, at least some of the time. Once Jess had stopped gloating about being right, their conversation returned to TV shows and music, and she managed to distract herself.

At other times it didn't work so well. On Sunday she woke up at four in the morning, drenched in sweat, her heart pounding from a nightmare in which Lauren's hair had blown aside to reveal that the whole back of her skull was covered in eyes. There were dozens of them, spreading like rot on old wood. Some were huge, some were small, but all were bloodshot and all were filled with hate.

It wasn't until History class the following Monday that Mia got really obsessed again. Savannah walked in with her left arm in a sling. She was with Lauren and Gabriella and they were in the middle of one of their muttered conversations.

"What happened?" asked Lucy Singh, who was sitting on the front row.

Savannah kept on murmuring to the others as though she hadn't heard. The Queens sat in their usual seats, two rows in front of Mia.

Mia gazed at Savannah's injury. She was convinced it had some link with the eyeball, but she couldn't work out what.

The teacher began the lesson, which was about a horrible plague in the fourteenth century, but Mia paid no attention. She was just staring at Savannah's sling. It was made from thick, padded blue nylon and had a strap that fixed over her right shoulder. There was a Velcro strip running along it, sealing it around her wrist.

As Mia studied it she noticed it was moving. At first it was just swaying slightly, but it soon began to jerk from side to side. If Savannah's arm was broken, she should have been wincing with pain. But she just seemed irritated.

It looked like there were tiny creatures inside, struggling to escape. Savannah pressed her free arm on the sling until it fell still.

It stayed that way for almost the whole lesson. But five minutes from the end it started moving again. This time it took Savannah by surprise and there was a small rip as the Velcro came apart.

Four thin strips of pink shot out. Savannah shoved them back in.

This time Mia was sure of what she'd seen. There were four fingers growing out of Savannah's wrist.

The first thing Mia felt was relief. This meant the eyeball was real too. She hadn't been imagining it. Then she was disgusted. The Queens weren't just a silly gang who didn't want to talk to anyone. They were doing something very wrong, maybe something evil.

Mia felt like ripping Savannah's sling away and showing everyone what was going on. But if she struck now she'd never find out what the Queens were up to. She needed to be patient.

Savannah didn't come in the next day. Mia looked out for her at the side of the Science block, but only Lauren and Gabriella were there.

In their Maths lesson that afternoon, Mia took her usual seat next to Jess and waited for the room to fill up.

"A quick warning," said Mia. "As soon as the lesson starts, I'm going to rush forwards and take the seat Savannah usually sits in."

"Please don't," said Jess. She put her bag of jelly babies down and grabbed Mia's arm. "You haven't lived down your last attempt to make friends with the Queens yet. I didn't want to say anything, but loads of people were talking about it."

"I don't care," said Mia. "I need to keep trying with them. I can't explain why just yet, but I'll tell you what all this is about soon."

Jess slumped forwards onto her hands.

"You don't need to explain," she said. "I know I'm just a temporary friend until you can move on to some better ones. It's happened before."

"It's not that at all," said Mia. "Trust me."

As soon as Mr Harris started the lesson Mia crept forwards and grabbed the spare seat next to Gabriella.

"How's Savannah's arm?" whispered Mia.

There was no response.

Lauren was on the other side of Gabriella. Mia leaned forwards and waved.

"Hey Lauren," said Mia. "Have you heard from Savannah today?"

Lauren didn't take her eyes off her exercise book.

Mia glanced over her shoulder. Jess was wincing. A couple of other students were looking at her and giggling.

She didn't care. She turned her attention back to Gabriella and Lauren.

"I'm just a little worried about her," said Mia. "Her injury looked pretty bad."

She kept her eyes on the girls, and right at the end of the lesson she spotted something.

Gabriella scratched her stomach, pulling the cloth of her jumper tight. There was an odd shape jutting out of her side.

Mia had to find out more about it, but there was no point asking Gabriella anything. She bent down and pretended to tie her shoelace. On the way back up she made herself fall sideways.

"Whoops!" she shouted.

She reached out to steady herself. She only felt the shape on Gabriella's side for an instant, but she knew exactly what it was.

Gabriella yelped and pushed her chair back across the floor with a metal scrape. She glared at Mia and rearranged her sweater.

"Sorry," said Mia. "My mistake."

Mia stared at Gabriella as she stormed out of the classroom. She knew what she'd felt. There was no mistaking it. Growing out of the side of Gabriella's body, hidden by her loose sweater, was a nose.

CHAPTER 3
SHE WILL KNOW

"Stop looking at them," said Jess. "Let it go."

It was lunchtime on Wednesday and the Queens were hanging around at the side of the Science block again. Savannah was back now, and her sling had gone, but there were four short, fresh scars along her arm.

Mia was standing a few metres away with Jess and staring at them.

"You've embarrassed yourself twice already," said Jess. "Don't tell me you're going to do it again."

Jess was eating Smarties by putting her mouth around the tube and tipping her head back. Mia wondered if she was even managing to chew them at all or was just swallowing some of them whole.

"No," said Mia. "I guess there's no point."

"And you'd have saved yourself double shame if you'd listened to me in the first place," said Jess through her mouthful of sweets.

"I still need to work out what they're up to," said Mia. "There's…"

She tailed off.

Jess had her head tipped back for another swig of Smarties. Mia wondered how much she could tell her.

"There's something wrong with them," said Mia.

"Of course there is," said Jess. "They won't speak to anyone. Rudeness like that isn't normal."

"It's not that," said Mia. "They're sort of…
weird looking."

Jess swallowed her sweets and stared at Mia in
confusion. "Firstly, no they're not. And secondly,
what would it matter if they were? So what if
someone looks a bit different?"

She tipped her head back to pour the last of the
Smarties in.

Mia shook her head. She didn't know how to
make herself clearer except to tell Jess everything.

"Savannah was growing four extra fingers out
of her wrist," said Mia. "That's why she had the
sling. They've been removed now."

Jess let her mouth fall open, revealing a mush of
half-chewed food.

"And Lauren had an eyeball growing under
her hair, but that's also gone now," said Mia.
"Gabriella has a nose growing from the side of
her body and I'm pretty sure that's still there.

I think they grow extra body parts and then get them taken off."

Jess crushed her Smarties tube and tossed it into a bin.

"OK," she said. "I don't think I'm really the person you should be talking to right now. Maybe if you see Mrs Lewis she can get you an appointment with a counsellor or something."

Mia flushed red. "You know what? It's fine. I shouldn't have said anything."

Jess reached out and placed her fingers around Mia's wrist. "You need help. And I want to see that you get it."

Mia dragged her hand away. "It's what I saw," she said. "You don't believe me and neither would anyone else. If I can find out a little bit more and maybe get some proof, I can tell other people what I've found. But right now I'm on my own."

Over by the Science block, the Queens were deep in one of their weird, muttered conversations.

"I'm not sure I should be encouraging you," said Jess. "But why don't you listen to them from inside the Science block? If you stood by the window you could probably hear what they were saying."

Mia looked over at the Queens. They were standing on the corner where a brick wall met a set of wide windows with white frames.

"You're right," said Mia. "I'll try tomorrow. You stand guard outside the classroom and keep the hall monitors away."

"Great," said Jess. "Even when I make friends with someone crazy, I still let them call the shots."

*

Mia made her way down to the Science block the following lunchtime. There was a year seven class filing out and she had to wait for them all to go.

Jess caught up with her while she waited. Her face was red from rushing down the stairs and she took a bottle of Pepsi out of her bag and drained most of it.

"Thanks for coming," said Mia. "If any hall monitors turn up, pretend you've lost your keys and ask for help. Don't let them into the classroom."

Jess sighed. "Yes boss."

Mia made her way over to the far corner of the classroom. She flattened herself against the wall beside the window.

She could hear distant shouting from the playground and Jess glugging her Pepsi in the corridor, but nothing else.

She focused on making her breathing as quiet as possible. If the Queens heard her, they'd leave their spot and she'd never get the chance to listen in on them again.

Mia heard footsteps outside. It was them.
They started talking, too low at first for Mia to
pick out any words or phrases. But eventually
she caught part of their discussion.

"We need to be faster," said Lauren.

"How?" asked Savannah.

"She will show us the way," said Lauren.

Gabriella was speaking too, but Mia couldn't
understand her at all. She was chanting under
her breath and it sounded like she was repeating
a prayer.

Mia was stiff with tension. She was sure that even
the smallest movement would give her away.

"Meet me on the allotments at dawn tomorrow,"
said Lauren. Her voice was louder and clearer
now. "We shall speak to her then."

Mia heard only a few more snippets. They kept

saying "she will know" and "let's ask her" but didn't give any clues about who this person was.

Gabriella was still chanting the same weird phrase. At the end of lunch break, Lauren and Savannah joined in. They were whispering too, but their voices were easier to understand.

"All hail the Queen of Flies," they were saying.

"All hail the Queen of Flies."

"All hail the Queen of Flies."

CHAPTER 4
THE FLIES

Mia stepped out of her house and pulled her front door closed. It made a loud click, but she couldn't hear any noise from inside. Her parents hadn't stirred.

She set off down the street. The sky was still dark except for a small blue strip on the horizon. Soon it would be dawn, the time the Queens had agreed to meet at the allotments. Mia was pretty sure they were talking about the land opposite the Civic Hall. It was split into small squares lined with rows of flowers and vegetables, broken up by old sheds. Gardeners were usually tending to their allotments, but none of them would be out yet.

Mia took the shortcut from the back of her estate to the main road, and soon wished she'd gone the long way round. There were no streetlamps in the narrow alleyway and she couldn't stop herself imagining dark figures in the shadows. Someone would step out holding a knife and demand her phone and purse, or maybe someone crazy would attack her just for the hell of it.

The words of the Queens came back to her:

All hail the Queen of Flies. All hail the Queen of Flies.

That's who Mia was heading towards. She had a sick feeling deep in her stomach. Something told her the Queen of Flies would be worse than any mugger or attacker.

Mia had begged Jess to come. She'd told her everything she'd overheard and said she was convinced the Queens were up to something bad. Jess had said she wouldn't come even if they were roasting puppies. Nothing would get her out of bed this early.

So she had come to face the girls and their Queen alone. Sweat ran down Mia's forehead as visions of this mysterious leader flashed into her mind. She imagined something slumped and hunched, with bulging eyes split into thousands of tiny sections. Suddenly she couldn't breathe.

Mia turned onto the high street and tried to get her breathing back under control. All she had to do was find out what the Queens were up to. She could get some photos on her phone, maybe even some video. Then she would hand them over to the police and let them deal with it.

She reached the allotments and peered over the low brick wall. Small streaks of orange were forming in the sky and things were becoming clearer. She could see nothing moving except for a plastic bag caught in a tree.

Mia looked around slowly, studying every scrap of land from the edge of the primary school to the backs of the houses on Lynton Avenue. Finally, she caught a murky shape moving in the far corner. It seemed to come into focus then disappear again.

She stepped through the allotments, tracing a zigzag path between rows of cabbages and sunflowers. As she got closer, she could see why the shape was shifting around so rapidly. It was a large swarm of flies buzzing around a shed.

They landed on her face and hands as she walked slowly towards the shed. She brushed them away, but she was sweating even more now which only drew in more of them.

She forced herself into the thick cloud of flies. Whatever the Queens had been arranging, this is where it was happening. The flies disgusted her, but she'd have to put up with them.

The buzzing was so loud it was unbearable. There was a rotting smell which Mia thought might be the flies, but as she approached the shed she knew it was coming from inside. It was a deep, bitter smell like old meat left outside on a hot day.

Sick rose up her throat and she had to swallow it. There was another noise under the buzzing now. A low moaning coming from the shed. The flies crawled into her ears and nostrils and covered her lips, but she kept going.

There was a square gap in the side of the small wooden building. Perhaps a window had once been there, but now it was just a hole surrounded by splintering wood. The inside was dark and filled with flies.

Mia brushed the insects aside in broad strokes and peered in. At first she could just see a thick, swirling wall of flies, but gaps appeared and let her glimpse what was there.

First she saw an arm. It was a human arm, but raw and sticky, as if it had no skin. It was gripping the end of a wooden armchair. There were four fingers on the right hand and Mia knew at once they were the ones she'd seen on Savannah's arm.

She saw a leg. It was the same soggy red mess broken up by small patches of skin.

Finally, the figure's head could be seen. It was a skull coated in meat and crawling flies. A low moan was coming from the lipless mouth. A nose jutted out in the middle and Mia was sure it was the one she'd felt under Gabriella's baggy sweater. The left eye socket was empty and dark, but there was a bloodshot blue eye in the other one. It gazed at Mia with hatred. The same way it had looked at her when she'd seen it under Lauren's hair.

Mia became aware of footsteps behind her. She turned to see Lauren, Savannah and Gabriella. They were all grinning and looking into her eyes now, even Gabriella.

"All hail the Queen of Flies," they said as one.

Mia could hear her pulse in her ears. It was getting louder and faster, drowning out the flies.

"Let me go," she said. "Let me go and I won't tell anyone about this."

She swallowed again. There was more than sick in her mouth this time. Some of the flies must have got in.

"All hail the Queen of Flies," said the others. "All hail the Queen of Flies."

They stepped towards her.

CHAPTER 5
ESCAPE

Mia screamed. Gabriella grabbed her left arm and Savannah took her right. She felt Lauren grab a handful of her hair and yank her head back.

"The Queen of Flies wants to meet you," said Lauren. "She's been looking forward to it so much."

They pushed her around the side of the shed and through the open door. The flies parted around them.

Mia could see the Queen of Flies clearly now. Most of her body was soft, red and slightly wet like old, uncooked steak. But there were patches

of skin on her stomach, thighs and shoulder. She let out another low, rasping moan.

"What is it?" Mia asked.

The rancid smell hit her nostrils. It was so strong it made her eyes water.

The girls lined up behind her, blocking the doorway.

"She's the Queen of Flies," said Lauren. "Bow before the Queen."

"I know you call it that," Mia said. "But what is it?"

"She comes from above and beyond," said Gabriella. "We've been helping her to become human so she can stay in this world."

Mia tried to process what she was hearing. This vile thing was some sort of alien who wanted to take human form, and the girls had been growing body parts to give to it. A voice deep in her mind told her to stop thinking about it and focus on survival. If she didn't get out soon, she'd be weak, easy prey for the monster in front of her.

"We grew some skin for her," said Lauren. "And we gave her so much blood it made us dizzy. But it still wasn't enough. Without you, we would have failed our Queen."

"What do you mean, without me?" asked Mia. "I didn't do anything."

"Yes you did," said Savannah. "You listened to our conversation yesterday and you took our invitation. We knew you were there."

The Queen of Flies let out a low cry.

"It was important to the Queen that you came of your own free will," said Gabriella. "She didn't want us to just drag someone in from the street. She wanted someone who had chosen to be here. You'll be making such an important sacrifice."

"What sacrifice?" asked Mia. "I haven't agreed to anything."

"You've had many chances to turn away," said Lauren. "Now you must make the Queen complete."

The small voice in Mia's mind became louder.

Stop talking to them. Stop trying to work out what all this means. Just run.

This time Mia listened. She spun around and charged for the door. Lauren, Savannah and Gabriella grasped at her, pulling her hair and her jumper, but she ducked and tore herself free.

She rushed outside into the swarm of flies. They whirled around her in tiny circles and she had to thrash her arms about to clear them. They swooped into her face and her eyeballs stung as they were scratched by tiny wings. She scrunched her eyes shut and pushed on.

Her head was pounding. The horrible smell and the noise of the insects were making her sick and unsteady.

The Queen of Flies was screaming behind her, letting out a deep cry like a cow in a slaughterhouse.

Someone grabbed Mia's wrists. She was afraid to open her eyes. Had her blind run somehow taken her in a circle and back into the grip of the Queens?

"Mia," said a familiar voice. "It's me."

She opened her eyes and a face became clear through the swirl of flies.

Jess.

"Oh, thank God you came," said Mia. Hot tears ran down from her red eyes. "You don't want to see what they're up to in there. We need to run, we need to get to the police."

Jess smiled but she kept her firm grip on Mia's wrists.

"Did you hear me?" asked Mia. "We need to go."

"You can't leave," whispered Jess. "Our Queen needs you. We're so pleased you're making this sacrifice. We love our Queen."

Mia felt the others grab her and drag her back to the shed.

Had Jess been in on it too? Of course she had! She'd been the one who suggested listening in on the others. They'd all been working together, tricking her into coming here and facing the foul monster they worshipped.

And what did they want her to sacrifice? A finger? An ear? A whole leg?

The small voice in her mind spoke up again.

Run. Escape. Survive. There's still time.

But it was no use. The Queens were pulling her back by her arms and hair, and now Jess was pushing her stomach, facing her and laughing.

The four of them were too strong. This time she would have to face the Queen of Flies.

CHAPTER 6
GOODBYE

Mia opened her eyes. She was still in the shed, but time had passed. Bright sunlight was streaming in through the window and the open door.

The open door. She could dash for it. She just needed to get her strength.

They were all there and they were all smiling at her. Lauren, Savannah, Gabriella and Jess. But where was the Queen of Flies?

She looked around with a huge effort. She was sitting in the wooden armchair the monster had been sitting in. She forced her numb hand up to her face. Her nose, lips and ears were all still there. Whatever they wanted to take, they hadn't done it yet.

A low voice buzzed into her mind:

I am the Queen of Flies. I came from above and beyond. This planet shall be my new home.

Mia tried to make herself leap up, but only managed to slump forwards. Jess pushed her back.

"Don't fight it," she said. "It won't be long now."

"What part of me did you take?" asked Mia. "What did you cut off for the Queen of Flies?"

"We didn't give her a part of you," said Jess. "We gave her all of you. She's taken over your body, now she's taking over your mind. Please give in. It will be so much easier for you."

"No, no, no!" cried Mia. Her thoughts were becoming slow and muddled.

"Goodbye Mia," said Jess. "You really need to go."

The buzzing voice came back into Mia's mind and drowned out everything else:

I am the Queen of Flies.
I am the Queen of Flies.
I am the Queen of Flies.

Her head flopped forwards and she fell still.

"We've done it," whispered Lauren. "I know we have."

"It's worked," said Savannah. "I can feel it."

"Please, please, please," said Jess. She had her hands over her heart and she was jumping up and down.

Mia's eyes opened. But they weren't her eyes any more. Mia was gone.

The Queen of Flies stood up from the chair.

"Well done," she said. Her voice was deeper and it had a low, buzzing echo. "You have all proved yourselves worthy."

"All hail the Queen of Flies," chanted the others.

The Queen of Flies stepped out of the shed and the others followed.

"Come," she said. "There's work to be done."

THE END

ABOUT THE AUTHOR

Tim Collins is originally from Manchester, but now lives near London. He is the author of over 70 books, including *Wimpy Vampire*, *Dorkius Maximus*, *Cosmic Colin* and the World's Worst series. He has won awards in the UK and Germany.

ABOUT THE ARTIST

James Lawrence hails from a faraway land of vikings and motorcyclcs. He spends his days drawing rad pictures and chugging ice tea.

He is the creator of the fantasy wrestling webcomic The Legend of La Mariposa.